Noah and his wife think a flood
might be coming, so they have built
a big boat called the Ark. They are
sailing around the world to rescue the
animals before it starts to rain.

Let's all go on an animal adventure!

For Joshua Mole
S.G.

For Tom
A.P.

Reading Consultant: Prue Goodwin, Lecturer in literacy and children's books

ORCHARD BOOKS
338 Euston Road, London NW1 3BH
Orchard Books Australia
Level 17/207 Kent Street, Sydney, NSW 2000

First published in 2011
First paperback publication in 2012

ISBN 978 1 40830 559 1 (hardback)
ISBN 978 1 40830 567 6 (paperback)

A CIP catalogue record for this book is available from the British Library.

1 3 5 7 9 10 8 6 4 2 (hardback)
1 3 5 7 9 10 8 6 4 2 (paperback)

Printed in China

Orchard Books is a division of Hachette Children's Books,
an Hachette UK company.

Pesky
Sharks!

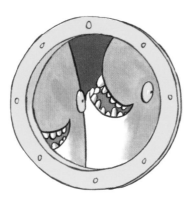

Written by Sally Grindley

Illustrated by Alex Paterson

ORCHARD BOOKS

It was a warm, clear night. Noah and
his wife were standing on the Ark in
their pyjamas. It was almost bedtime.
"Look at the stars twinkling,"
said Noah.

"They're very pretty," said Mrs Noah.

Noah began to sing. "*Twinkle, twinkle,*

little star!" He was very out of tune.

He sounded like a cat yowling!

"Shh, Noah," said Mrs Noah.

"You'll frighten the animals."

"My singing isn't that bad!" said Noah.

"Oh, yes it is," smiled Mrs Noah.

Just then, there was a loud bang on

the side of the Ark.

"What on earth was that?" said Noah.

Noah fetched his special torch with its extra long beam. He shone it over the side of the Ark.

Suddenly, a great white shark leapt out of the water. The shark grinned a wide toothy grin, then landed again with an enormous splash!

"He's got my pyjamas all wet!"
moaned Noah.

The shark leapt out of the water
again.

"He's trying to come
on board!" cried Mrs Noah.
"Tell him we're very sorry,
but we haven't got room
for fish."

Noah leant over the side of the Ark.
"Shoo, shoo!" he shouted. "We're
very sorry, but we haven't got
room for fish!"

The shark whacked his tail against
the Ark and swam away.

"He's gone," said Noah.

"Phew," said Mrs Noah. "I thought he
was going to wake up all the animals."

Mr and Mrs Noah went to bed.
Just as they were drifting off to sleep,
there was another bang on the side of
the Ark.

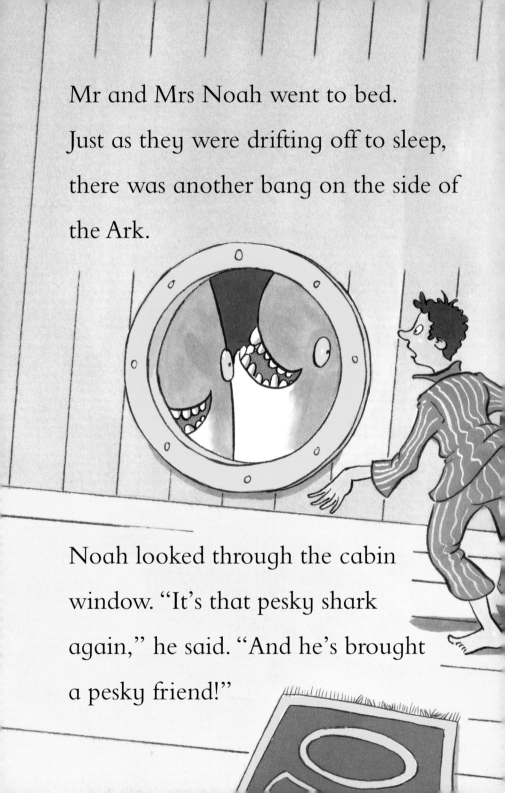

Noah looked through the cabin
window. "It's that pesky shark
again," he said. "And he's brought
a pesky friend!"

Two sharks grinned their toothy
grins at them.

Noah opened the
window. "Shoo!"
he shouted. "We're
trying to sleep."
The first shark
sprayed him with
water.

The other whacked the Ark with his tail.

Suddenly, there was a tiny *eek!*
followed by lots of squeals.
"Now look what you've done,"
Mrs Noah grumbled. "You've woken
the mice and the guinea pigs!"

There was a loud *baaa!* followed by
lots of growls.
"And now you've woken the sheep
and the bears," grumbled Noah.

"You naughty sharks," said Mrs Noah. "We'll never get them back to sleep now."
The sharks waggled their tails cheekily.

They swam to the other side of the
Ark and banged on it again.

All over the Ark, the animals
began to wake up.

WOOF! barked the dogs.

MEOW!
went the cats.

GRRRR!
growled the
lions and tigers.

MOOOO!
went the cows.

CLUCK CLUCK!
went the chickens.

Noah and his wife ran from one part of the Ark to another.

"Shh! Shh!" they said to the animals.

"Go back to sleep."

They tickled the foxes . . .

They stroked the rabbits . . .

They scratched the elephants . . .

They patted
the badgers . . .

They gave apples to the donkeys
and zebras . . .

But every time the animals settled
down, the sharks knocked on the
Ark again.

"What are we going to do?" said
Noah.

"I have an idea," said Mrs Noah.
She went to a cupboard and took out
a megaphone.

"Sing to the sharks, Noah," she said.

Noah frowned, but he did as he was told. He took the megaphone and began to sing *The Animals Went In Two By Two*.

Mrs Noah put her fingers in her ears. All over the Ark, the animals howled and moaned and wailed even more loudly than before.

As soon as the sharks heard Noah,
they looked at each other in horror.
They dived back under the water and
swam away from the Ark as fast as
they could go.

"Well done, Noah!" cried Mrs Noah as she watched the sharks disappear. "Your singing made them go away!"

The rest of the animals soon settled down.